the HICCUPotamus

This book is for Amity
(who makes my heart bam-bamity)

the HICCUPotamus

by Aaron Zenz

two lions

Hic!

Hic!

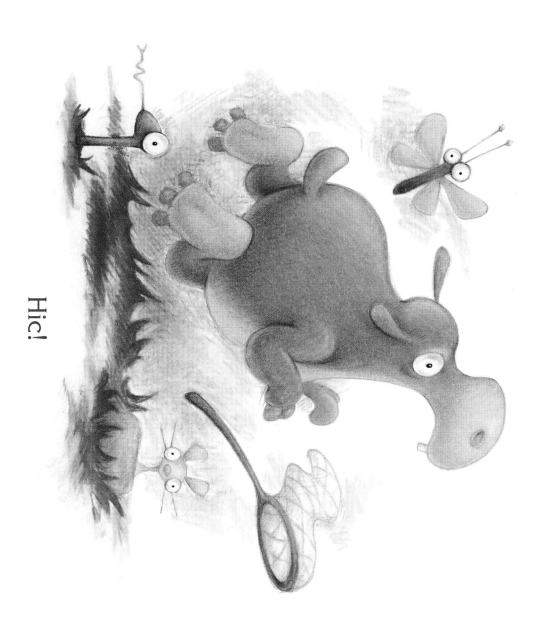

There was a hippopotamus
Who hiccupped quite-a-lotamus
And every time he got'emus . . . .

. . . He'd fall upon his bottomus.

One day he saw an elephant
With cakes of green and yellowphant.

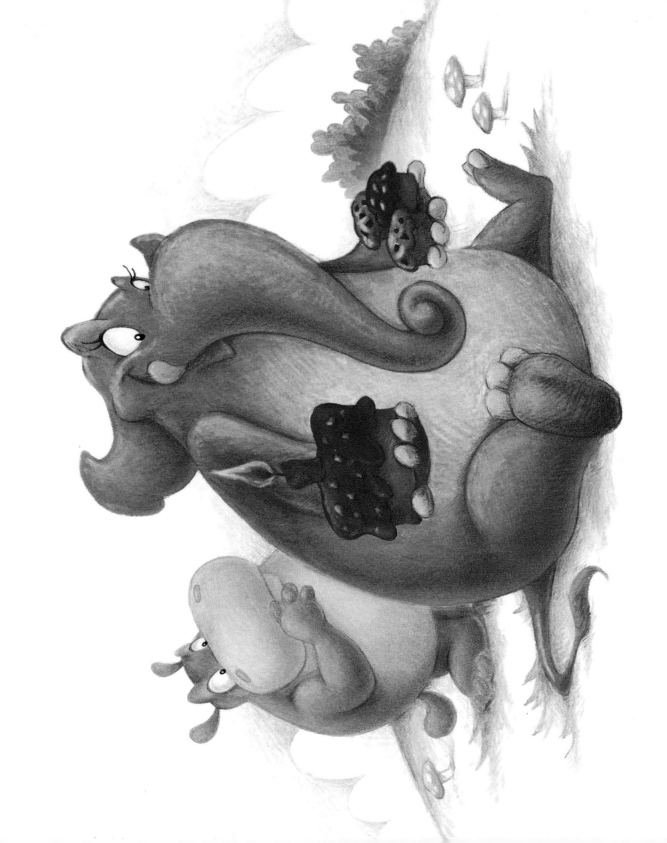

He tried to tell her "hellophant" . . .

. . . But it didn't go so wellephant.

She chased him toward a centipede
Pouring new cementipede.

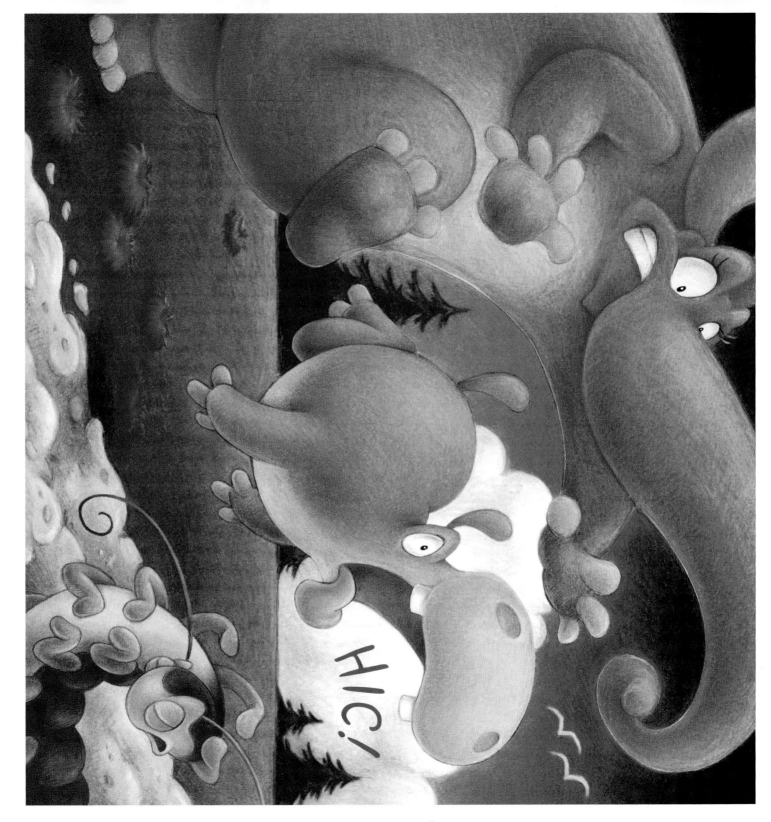

He hic'ed by accidentipede . . . .

. . . And tripped the elephantipede.

They ran near a rhinoceros
With minty dental flosserous.

His string went all criss-crosserous . . .

. . . And *that* was the last strawcerous.

They tried to find a therapy –
Some cure which they could shareapy,
A what or why or whereapy
To stop this long nightmareapy.

So . . .

They wrapped him 'round with licorice
And spun him very quickerish.

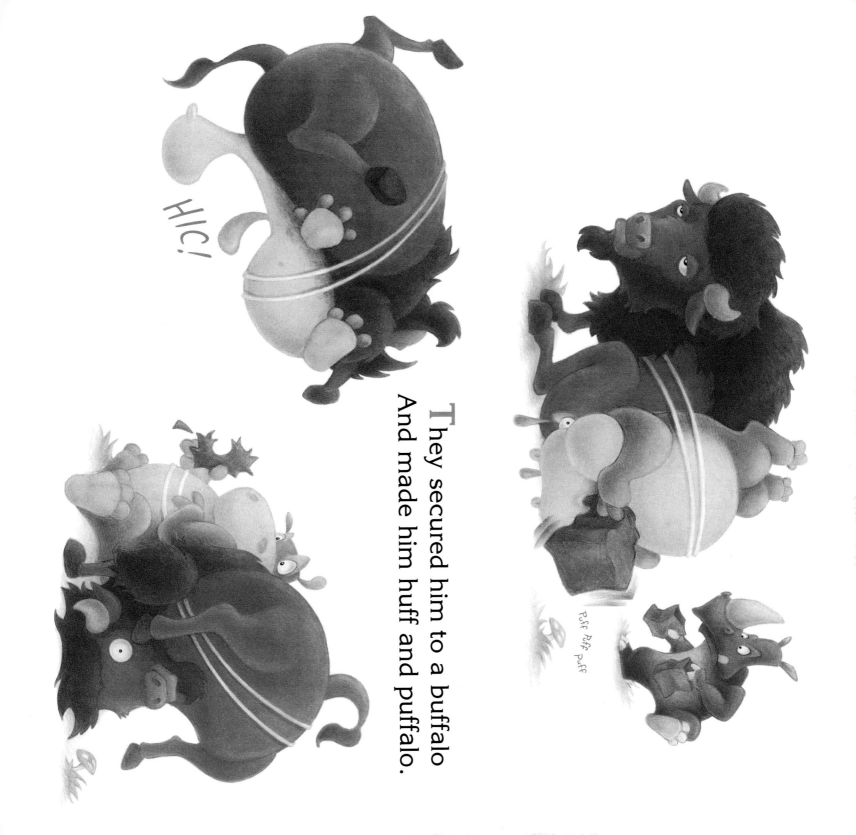

They secured him to a buffalo
And made him huff and puffalo.

They acquired an aquarium
And flashed him something scaryum.

They poured him tubs of vinegar
And tickled his chinny-chin-chinigar.

HIC!

And then at last – a miracle!
His hiccups, so severeacle,
Just didn't reappearacle!
He grinned from ear to earacle.

Until . . .

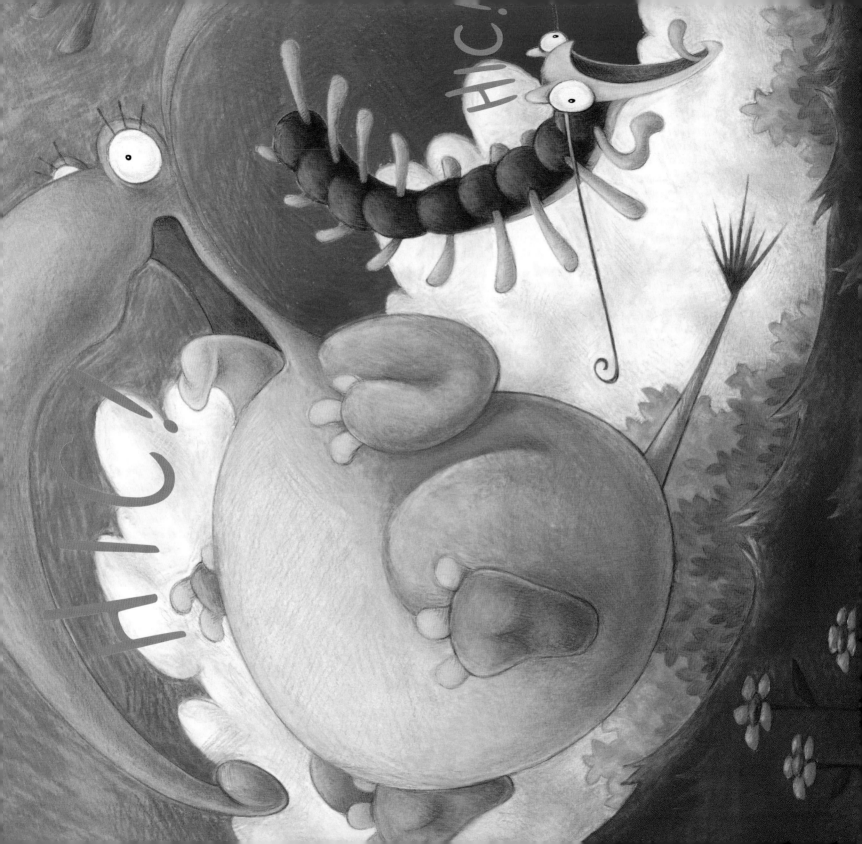

Cast Bios

The part of the Hiccupotamus was played by veteran hippo actor Hank Polowski. Due to a paralyzing fear of fish, some of his scenes in this book were performed by a crew of stunt doubles.

Bartholomew Poppins has appeared in over 100 roles in his picture book career. He still dreams of landing a leading part, but is proud of his work in *The Hiccupotamus* and his cameo as "something squishy" in *Mr. Binkers Steps in Something Squishy*.

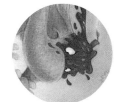

Many considered it a risk casting an unknown in the significant elephant role. But it would appear that pachyderm Katie McMurphy has a promising career ahead of her. Following a serious allergic reaction, however, she is currently turning down all parts that involve the use of frosting.

Samu Ti speaks no English, which created occasional confusion during his work on *The Hiccupotamus*. Author Aaron Zenz recalls the time the script called for the centipede to pour cement, but instead Samu began purring like a cat. "The more I shouted 'Pour! Pour! Pour!' the louder he'd purr!"

This is the final role for Dennis Flott. He is retiring to a small bee-keeping community in North Western Idaho. Good luck, Dennis! We wish you all the best.

The part of the buffalo was played by a ground squirrel named Arlo. It took 14 hours in the make-up chair to get him ready each day. Unfortunately, that continually made for a very short window of opportunity to use him in costume.

two lions

First published in 2005 by Dogs in Hats Children's Publishing

All rights reserved
Amazon Publishing
Attn: Amazon Children's Publishing
P.O. Box 400818
Las Vegas, NV 89140
www.amazon.com/amazonchildrenspublishing

Library of Congress Cataloging-in-Publication Data
Zenz, Aaron.
The hiccupotamus / by Aaron Zenz. — 1st ed.
  p. cm.
Summary: A hippopotamus with severe hiccups causes chaos until
other creatures finally find the right cure.
ISBN 978-0-7614-5622-3
[1. Stories in rhyme. 2. Hiccups—Fiction. 3. Hippopotamus—Fiction.
4. Animals—Fiction. 5. Humorous stories.] I. Title.
PZ8.3.Z42Hic 2009
[E]—dc22   2008051334

The artwork was created entirely in colored pencil.

Printed in China
13